Wibble Wobble

For Finn
M M

For my Mum and best friend –
thanks for EVERYTHING
J M

ORCHARD BOOKS
338 Euston Road, London NW1 3BH
Orchard Books Australia
Hachette Children's Books
Level 17/207 Kent Street, Sydney, NSW 2000
ISBN 1 84121 086 2
13 digit ISBN 9781841210865
First published in Great Britain in 2001
First paperback publication in 2002
Text © Miriam Moss 2001
Illustrations © Joanna Mockler 2001
The rights of Miriam Moss to be identified as the author
and of Joanna Mockler to be identified as the illustrator
of this work have been asserted by them in accordance with
the Copyright, Designs and Patents Act, 1988.
A CIP catalogue record for this book is available from the British Library.
5 7 9 10 8 6
Printed in China

Wibble Wobble

by Miriam Moss

illustrated by Joanna Mockler

ORCHARD BOOKS

All William ever wanted in the whole world
was to have a **wobbly** tooth.

Everyone else in his class had one.
Louie's twisted round and round
and Rosa's lay flat on its back.

But William's teeth seemed stuck,
superglued to his gums.

"It isn't fair," said William. "Everyone else at school tells **wobbly** tooth stories."

"When your wobbly tooth
comes out, Gran," said William,
"you get a silver coin from
the Tooth Fairy."

"Is that so?" said Gran.
"Yes," said William. "And if it comes out at
school, you have to keep it somewhere safe."

"Vita stuck hers to the velcro on her trainers...

and Christie hid his in the cotton-wool in his ear.

AND...

today Nadir's got lost up her nose.

Mrs King said she'd keep them safe from now on."

The next day in quiet time, William
felt one of his teeth move at last!
"Mrs King!" he cried.
"My tooth moved! I felt it!"

William pushed his tooth forwards with his
tongue then sucked it back for Mrs King to see.
"Look, Rosa!" he said.
"Look, Louie!"

Push, pull,
jiggle, joggle.

Poke, flick,
wibble,
wobble.

"Come on, William," called Mum at bedtime.
"How long does it take to brush your teeth?"
"A long time," said William.
"It hurts my **wobbly** tooth."

William just couldn't leave his **wobbly** tooth alone.

Push, pull, jiggle, joggle.
Poke, flick, wibble,
wobble.

"Look, Louie," said William the next day,
twisting his tooth round and round.
"Look, Rosa," he said, as it lay flat on its back.

By bedtime William's tooth was hanging on one thin little thread.

Push, pull, jiggle, joggle.
Poke, flick, wibble, wobble.

Suddenly, the tooth flipped upside down and got stuck!

"Ow! Ow!" yelled William, jumping out of bed.
"Mum! Dad!" he cried, rushing downstairs.

Gently Dad turned the tooth back the right way up.
"Why doesn't it just come out?" said William.
"Don't worry," said Dad. "It will."

In PE the next day William did his best ever
spinning somersault. And when he stood up,
his tooth was sitting on his tongue!
William took it out and looked at it.
How tiny it was!

"Shall I look after it until home time?" asked Mrs King, wrapping it in a tissue and putting it on top of the filing cabinet.

"Then can I take it home?" asked William, feeling a bit **wobbly** himself.

"Of course you can," said Mrs King.

That afternoon, William sat poking his tongue
into the hole in his gum, waiting for Louie
to finish vegetable printing.
Suddenly, "Aaargh!" shouted Louie,
dancing about. "I've got chilli in my eye!"
"I'll get a tissue, Mrs King," said Rosa.

Mrs King dabbed Louie's eye and before long it was home time.

"Look, Mum!" William said.
"My tooth came out!"
"Oh, William!" said Mum.
"Can I see it?"
"It's on the filing cabinet,
wrapped up in a tissue,"
said William.
"Here it is," said Mrs King.
Then, "Oh! It's gone."

They searched everywhere.
Suddenly William stopped.
"Rosa gave Louie a tissue," he said,
"when he got red hot chilli in his eye."
Mum and Mrs King looked at each other.

"Don't worry William," said Mum,
searching in the bin. "We'll find it."

William sat down
and stared at his feet.
He was missing his tooth
really badly now.
He was sure they'd
never find it.

Suddenly, Mum stood up. "This might be it!"
She unwrapped the tissue – and there was
William's tooth!

Mrs King washed the tooth and gave it back to William. "Perhaps the Tooth Fairy will leave something a bit special tonight," said Mrs King. "After all that."

The next morning William
looked under his pillow.
There lay a little wooden box.
He lifted the lid and inside
was a shiny silver coin!

When William got to school he told
everyone his **w o b b l y** tooth story.
"I expect you'd like a rest
from **w o b b l y** teeth for a while,
William!" said Mrs King.
"Yes," said William.
"I would!"

On the way home from school,
William took his silver coin
and bought the most
enormous ice-cream.

It had little coloured sweets stuck all over it, layers
of chocolate, and chewy toffee in the middle.

William unwrapped
it and took a big bite.
Ping!
went the little
coloured sweets.
Crack!
went the chocolate.
Squelch!
went the ice-cream.
Crunch!
went the ice-cold,
rock-hard toffee . . .
and guess what?

Another tooth wobbled!

Push, pull, jiggle, joggle.

poke, flick,

wibble,

wobble.